Where to, Little Wombat?

Charles Fuge

WALKER BOOKS

AND SUBSIDIARIES

LONDON • BOSTON • SYDNEY • AUCKLAND

THIS WALKER BOOK BELONGS TO:

- -

- -

- -

For Lucy
C.F.

This edition published 2022 by Walker Books Ltd
87 Vauxhall Walk, London SE11 5HJ

2 4 6 8 10 9 7 5 3 1

First published 2006 by Gullane Children's Books

© 2006 Charles Fuge

The right of Charles Fuge to be identified as author of this work has been asserted
in accordance with the Copyright, Designs and Patents Act 1988

This book has been typeset in Didact Gothic and Love Ya Like a Sister

Printed in China

British Library Cataloguing in Publication Data:
a catalogue record for this book is available from the British Library

ISBN 978-1-5295-0577-1

www.walker.co.uk

Mum was spring-cleaning the burrow.
"I wish we could live somewhere more
exciting," grumbled Little Wombat.
"I'm bored of burrows."

"Well then," said Mum. "Why don't
you go and and see if you
can find somewhere better?"
She wanted to get on.

Koala was up
his gum tree
eating leaves.

"Can I live with you?"
asked
Little Wombat.

Koala thought it
was a cool idea ...

but
wombats
aren't built
to climb
trees!

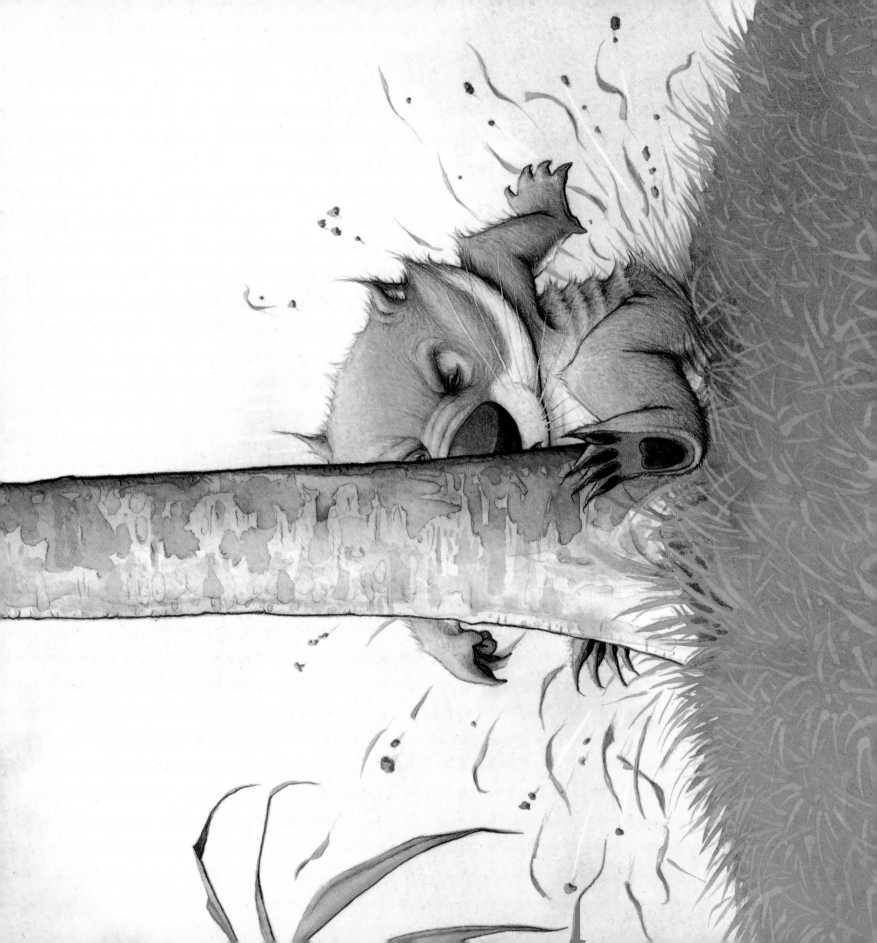

Frog was resting on his favourite lily pad.

"Can I live with you?" asked Little Wombat.
Frog thought it was a fantastic idea ...

but wombats are too
heavy to walk on lily pads!

Mole was digging new tunnels as usual.
"Can I live with you?" asked Little Wombat.

Mole thought it was
a marvellous idea ...

but wombats are much
bigger than moles!

Tortoise was asleep inside his shell.

"No room here!"

But the ants knew of a
great big nest nearby.

Little Wombat was just making
himself comfortable ...

when angry Mrs Emu appeared
and shooed him away!

Little Wombat arrived home
looking sorry for himself.
"So you didn't find anywhere
then?" said Mum kindly.

"Never mind," she smiled. "Burrows are best!
And ours is nice and tidy with lots of room!"
And to prove it, she said he could
have all his friends round for a sleepover.